Dear Parents,

Welcome to the Scholastic Reader series. We have taken over 80 years of experience with teachers, parents, and children and put it into a program that is designed to match your child's interests and skills.

Level 1—Short sentences and stories made up of words kids can sound out using their phonics skills and words that are important to remember.

Level 2—Longer sentences and stories with words kids need to know and new "big" words that they will want to know.

Level 3—From sentences to paragraphs to longer stories, these books have large "chunks" of text and are made up of a rich vocabulary.

Level 4—First chapter books with more words and fewer pictures.

It is important that children learn to read well enough to succeed in school and beyond. Here are ideas for reading this book with your child:

- Look at the book together. Encourage your child to read the title and make a prediction about the story.
- Read the book together. Encourage your child to sound out words when appropriate. When your child struggles, you can help by providing the word.
- Encourage your child to retell the story. This is a great way to check for comprehension.

Scholastic Readers are designed to support your child's efforts to learn how to read at every age and every stage. Enjoy helping your child learn to read and love to read.

—**Francie Alexander**
Chief Education Officer
Scholastic Education

Written by Kristin Earhart with consultation by Joanna Cole.

Based on *The Magic School Bus* books written by Joanna Cole and illustrated by Bruce Degen.

The author and editor would like to thank Paula Mikkelsen of the American Museum of Natural History, New York City, for her expert advice in preparing this manuscript.

Illustrated by Carolyn Bracken.

0-439-68403-X

20 19 40 16 17 18 19/0

Designed by Rick DeMonico.

Printed in the U.S.A.
First printing, April 2005

The Magic School Bus®
GETS CRABBY

SCHOLASTIC INC.

New York Toronto London Auckland Sydney
Mexico City New Delhi Hong Kong Buenos Aires

It's fun to be in Ms. Frizzle's class.
ANEMONE
DA

She wears funny dresses.
She wears funny shoes.

We have been learning about where different animals live.
But today we are going to the pool.
I CAN'T WAIT TO GO TO THE POOL!
MAYBE THE FRIZ WILL GIVE US SWIMMING LESSONS.

Ms. Frizzle says it's time to leave.

Ms. Frizzle drives right past the swimming pool.
We drive for a long time.
POOL
WAIT!
MS. FRIZZLE, YOU MISSED IT!
BYE, POOL!

When we stop, we are by the ocean.
The water is coming in and going out.
WOW!
AT MY OLD SCHOOL, WE NEVER WENT TO A POOL LIKE THIS.
HIGH AND LOW
by Ralphie
The ocean water comes up to the land in waves. At times, the waves do not come up very far on the land. This is called low tide.
After low tide, the waves start to go higher. When they are at the highest point, it is called high tide.

As the tide goes out,
we see more of the beach.
Waves crash against rocks far away.
Ms. Frizzle drives toward them.

The Friz pushes a big button.
The bus starts to change.
It shrinks.
It grows eight legs and two claws.
Now it is the bus-crab!

The bus-crab climbs up on the rocks.
It crawls until it comes to a hole.
The hole is deep, but there is
water at the bottom.
CLASS, THIS IS A TIDE POOL!
ACCORDING TO MY RESEARCH, LOTS OF PLANTS AND ANIMALS LIVE HERE.
POOL
SEA PALM
BARNACLES
SEA ANEMONES
MUSSELS
SEA STAR
SEA SPONGE
SEA LETTUCE

Our bus-crab walks on the dry rocks.
"What are those?" Wanda asks.
"Those shells are animals," the Friz says.
"They are called barnacles."

The bus-crab jumps into the pool.
When we hit the bottom,
Ms. Frizzle tells us to get out.
We start to change as soon as we
leave the bus.
NOW WE ARE CRABS, TOO!
WE ARE HERMIT CRABS.

WE CAN BREATHE UNDERWATER.
CRABS HAVE GILLS, JUST LIKE FISH.
SHELL STANDS FOR SHELTER
by Keesha
Hermit crabs have soft bodies. They need shells to keep safe. They usually live in snail shells.

Ms. Frizzle tells us to explore.
We walk around on our four front legs.
Our back four legs stay inside our shell.

Just then, a shadow falls over us.
All we can see is green.
“Dead man’s fingers!” D.A. yells.
YIKES!
A DEAD MAN?
WHERE?

D.A. tells us not to worry.
"Dead man's fingers is not
a monster," she says.
"It's just a plant."
We feel better, but not for long.
THE TIDE IS COMING IN!
THE WATER IS MOVING!

IT'S HARD TO SEE!
WHERE DID ARNOLD GO?

BARNACLES
GIANT GREEN ANEMONE
MUSSELS
AT HIGH TIDE . . .
. . . THE TIDE POOL COMES TO LIFE!
WET IS BEST
by Wanda
At low tide, animals protect themselves from drying out. They close their shells and tentacles to keep water inside. When the tide rises, the animals open up again.
CLOSED
OPEN
SEA ANEMONE

We have to find Arnold!
We do not see him,
but we see lots of changes.
SLENDER-RAYED STAR
SEA LETTUCE

The water rushes all around us.
We see something float by.
It is Arnold's shell!
OH, NO!

WHAT HAPPENED TO ARNOLD?

We search all around.
We look up to the top of the pool.
The waves crash against the rocks.
The shells we saw before are now open.
ARE THOSE BARNACLES STICKING THEIR TONGUES OUT AT US?
ACTUALLY, THOSE LONG STRINGY THINGS ARE THEIR LEGS.
SUPER GLUE
by Keesha
Acorn barnacles make a special glue. They glue themselves to the rocks. The glue holds them in place so the waves won't carry them away.

MY RESEARCH SAYS THE BARNACLES USE THEM TO CATCH FOOD.
MY MOM WOULD NEVER LET ME EAT WITH MY FEET!

Then we see something bright and striped.
It is heading toward us!
It's Arnold!
ARNOLD, WE SAW YOUR OLD SHELL!
WHAT HAPPENED?

THAT SHELL WAS TOO SMALL, SO I FOUND A NEW ONE!
MOVING ON UP
by Arnold
Hermit crabs grow. As a crab grows, its shell can get tight. When a shell gets too small, the crab moves into a bigger one.

We climb back on the bus-crab.
All at once, we are kids again.
We drive across the sand and watch
the tide go out.

I BET THOSE BARNACLES ARE CLOSING UP SO THEY STAY WET.
I'M HAPPY TO BE NICE AND DRY.
SEA YA

We are happy to be back at school.
A lot happens in Ms. Frizzle's class,
but even more happens in tide pools.
Who knows what our next field trip
will bring?
NEXT UNIT:
MS. FRIZZLE HAS ON A NEW DRESS AGAIN.
DINO-MITE!

The Tide Zones

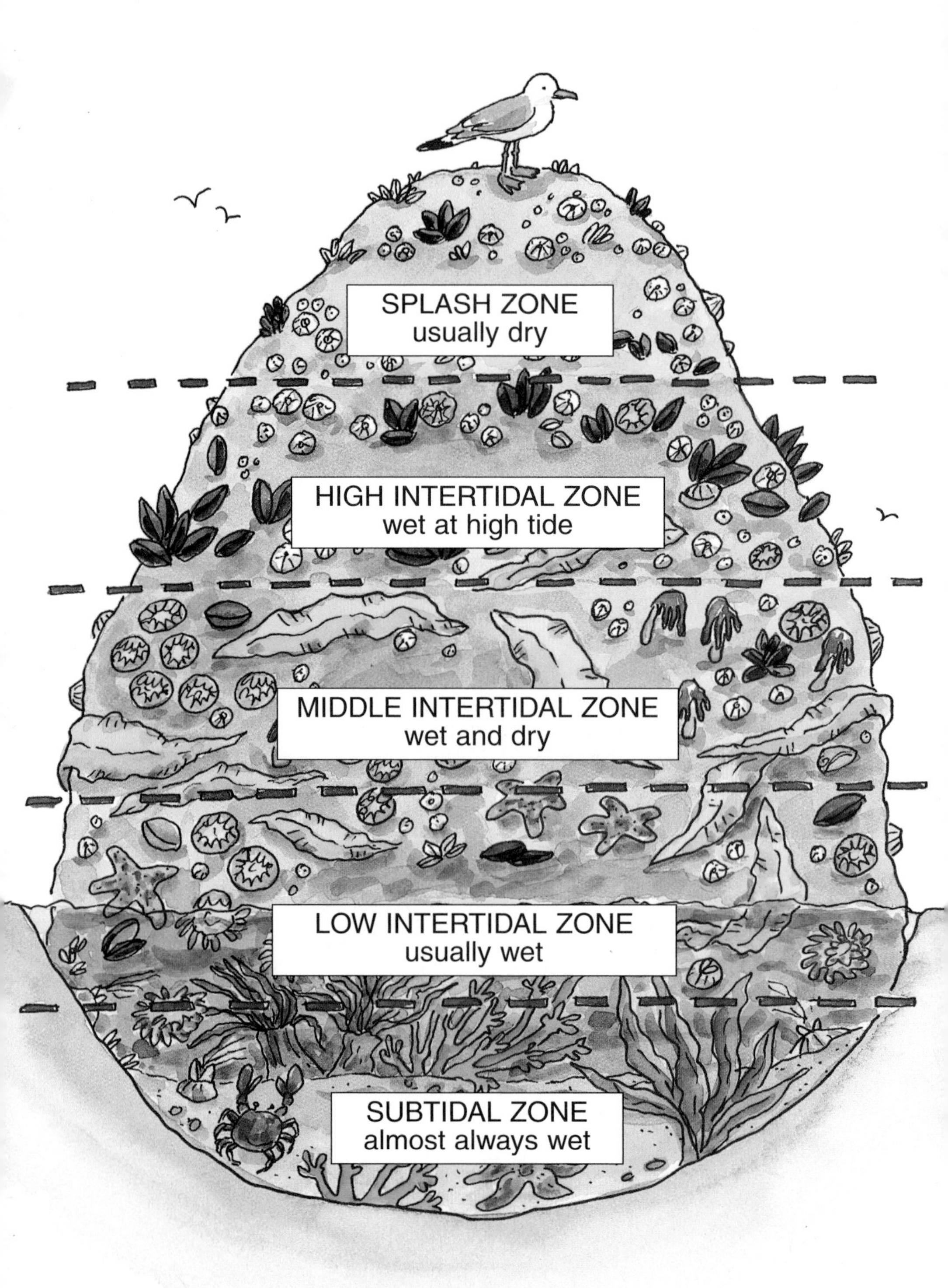